The LONE RANGER

By Steffi Fletcher
Illustrated by E. Joseph Dreany

A GOLDEN BOOK • NEW YORK

Educators and librarians, for a variety of teaching tools, visit us at RHTeachersLibrarians.com
Library of Congress Control Number: 2012945290
ISBN 978-0-449-81793-3
Printed in the United States of America
10 9 8 7 6

Young Tom Mason sat and hugged his knees. He was waiting for the stagecoach to thunder down the dusty road near his home. He wanted to wave to the stagecoach driver, Bill Mason. Bill was his big brother.

"And the best driver in all Texas!" Tom told himself proudly.

At last Tom heard the swift pounding of hooves.
The stagecoach careened around the bend. Tom
jumped to his feet, waving and smiling.

Then the smile on his face died.

"Bill!" he thought. "Where's Bill?"

The driver's seat was empty! The reins flapped
loosely on the horses' backs. The horses were
running away, their eyes wide with terror.

Without thinking, Tom raced into the road.

"Whoa! Whoa!" he shouted, and leaped for the lead horse's bit. With all his strength, he dragged at the horse's head.

The stagecoach slowed and stopped. Tom scrambled up to the driver's seat. A piece of bright material caught his eye—part of Bill's shirt!

"Something awful's happened!" he whispered.

He jumped off the coach and ran desperately toward his house.

"Pa! Pa!" he shouted. "Come quick!"

And then Tom remembered. His father had gone
to town, and he was all alone.

He would have to find Bill by himself, and help
him if he was in trouble.

Tom set off down the road at a steady lope.

Meanwhile, not far from Tom, the Lone Ranger and Tonto were riding by. They heard Tom's frightened shouts.

"Listen, Tonto!" the Lone Ranger cried. "That youngster's in trouble!"

They spurred their horses and met Tom on the road. Tom's face brightened when he saw the masked man on the big silver horse.

"The Lone Ranger!" he breathed. "It sure is lucky you came!"

Tom quickly told the Lone Ranger and Tonto about the runaway stagecoach.

The Lone Ranger lifted Tom onto his horse, Silver. "Let's take a look," he said. Followed by Tonto, they galloped off.

They had not ridden far before Tom gave a
frightened gasp.

"Look! Look there!" he cried.

A figure lay sprawled facedown in the road.

Tom slid off Silver and ran to kneel beside the still figure.

"Bill!" he cried. "Bill, are you hurt bad?"

Bill groaned. Gently the Lone Ranger helped him turn over. He had a bruise on his forehead.

"Who did it?" asked the Lone Ranger.

"A gang," said Bill. "They got on as passengers."

"Why?"

"Gold. I was carrying gold to the Yucca City Bank," Bill answered.

Bill raised himself up. He pointed.

"They headed that way," he whispered. "Better get a posse."

The Lone Ranger frowned thoughtfully.

"No," he said. "There isn't time. Tonto, you and Tom take Bill into Yucca City. I'll go after the gang."

Tom jumped to his feet. "Oh, please!" he begged. "Let me go with you!"

For a long moment the Lone Ranger looked at Tom. Then he nodded. "Okay, pardner," he said. "Guess it's your fight as much as mine."

They helped Bill up onto Tonto's horse, and Tonto and Bill set off for Yucca City. Tom and the Lone Ranger, mounted on Silver, headed the other way.

The Lone Ranger and Tom soon found the trail of the holdup men.

"They're on foot!" the Lone Ranger said. "We'll catch up with them soon."

But suddenly he stopped. With a grunt of disgust, he pointed down. The ground was rough and trampled.

"Horses! They had horses waiting for them! Looks like we'll have some hard riding to do."

For many hours Tom and the Lone Ranger rode in pursuit. They clattered up rocky hillsides, where the sparks flew from under Silver's hoofs.

They splashed across a wide river, where the water ran fierce and swift around Silver's legs.

"We're in luck, Tom!" the Lone Ranger exclaimed. "The river's in flood, or those varmints might have ridden downstream and shaken us off their trail!"

The sun hung red on the horizon when the Lone Ranger drew rein. Up ahead, a thread of smoke rose into the evening air.

"That may not be their fire," the Lone Ranger said. "But if it is, those varmints are mighty sure of themselves. Let's check."

He and Tom left Silver. On hands and knees they crawled forward and peered through the bushes.

Around a campfire four men were sitting. Beside the men lay the stolen bags of gold!

"Listen, Boss," one of the men was complaining. "I don't like this. We should be making tracks."

"Take it easy, Shorty," said the big man called Boss. "That stage still isn't due in Yucca City. We'll be safe across the border before it's missed."

The Lone Ranger stepped forward.

"Afraid not, mister," he said. "Afraid you'll be in jail." The holdup men jumped to their feet.

"Reach!" the Lone Ranger commanded, and their hands went into the air.

"Okay, Tom," the Lone Ranger ordered. "Get their guns."

Tom collected the guns. Then he helped the Lone Ranger tie the men to their horses. The Lone Ranger and Tom led the holdup men to Yucca City and turned them over to the sheriff.

When the bandits were safe in jail, the Lone Ranger and Tom carried the bags of gold to the Yucca City Bank.

The bank manager clapped Tom on the back.

"Bill came in and told us about the holdup," he said. "The doc's patched him up fine, and he's as good as new."

"Then I guess our job is done," said the Lone Ranger with a smile. "I'll find Tonto and move along. Thanks for your help, pardner!" he told Tom. And lifting his hand in farewell, the Lone Ranger leaped onto Silver and galloped away into the dusk.